Jambo, Sungura
Tales from East Africa

Jambo, Sungura
Tales from East Africa

by Eleanor B. Heady

illustrated by
Robert Frankenberg

W · W · NORTON & COMPANY INC · NEW YORK

To Harold,
for his never-failing encouragement

Contents

Preface

Stories of the hare are common in East Africa. Why such a small, timid animal should be endowed by story tellers with cunning, slyness and wisdom is a mystery. Perhaps it is because of the very human tendency to cheer the underdog.

Africans are gifted storytellers, often acting out their tales with dramatic movements and startling vocal sounds, including snatches of song, the roars of lions and noises of other animals.

East Africa, embracing the countries of Kenya, Uganda, Tanganyika and the island of Zanzibar, is occupied by many tribes. In former times these people spoke various languages. Hundreds of years ago there emerged a common language, Swahili, which spread inland over the trade routes, as the people of the coast bartered with their neighbors to the west. The tribal languages continued to be used, but Swahili became a second tongue of the majority. This common language helped to spread stories from tribe to tribe, so that the same or similar tales may now be heard in far distant parts of the land. Trade and wars between tribes added to this exchange, so that the stories of the farming Kikuyus were heard by the campfires of the Luo fishermen on the shores of Lake Victoria or a wandering Masai told his son a Kipsigi animal story as they herded cattle on the plains.

East Africa is a land of great variety, rising from the steaming hot Indian Ocean to the towering nineteen thousand, seven hundred foot peak of Mt. Kilimanjaro in Tanganyika. The Kenya highlands around snow-capped Mt. Kenya are on the equator, but have a temperate climate, even very cool at times. The highland people were farmers and hunters. The coast and lakeside dwellers fished and farmed, while those between usually lived by herding flocks of cattle and goats on the vast grasslands. The stories they told revolved around the pursuits of their daily lives. Since the hare is a common animal in all of East Africa, stories concerning him were popular with many groups of people.

These stories are all adaptations of originals. There are many versions of most of them. I have tried to choose the most interesting, sometimes adding to or subtracting from some of the stories as told in Africa. In all cases, African, mostly Swahili, names have been used and African customs and backgrounds have been kept authentic.

During the year I lived in East Africa, I asked

everyone I met for stories. Many people knew a few or gave me an idea or two. Librarians at the McMillan Memorial Library in Nairobi were most helpful, giving the free use of their excellent collection of books and papers on Africa. I am deeply indebted to the many anthropologists who have recorded the folkways of the various tribes, and to the host of friends and acquaintances who shared their stories with me.

Readers may, at first, find the African words difficult to pronounce. This explanation should help. Always accent next to the last syllable in any word. The consonants are pronounced as in English. The letter y is always a consonant. The beginning m or n is pronounced very slightly with a humming sound. Vowels are pronounced as follows: a as in father; e as the a in say; i as the ee in see; o as in go; and u as the oo in food. There are never any variations.

"Jambo" is a common greeting in most of east and central Africa. It is a friendly word, always spoken with a smile and usually with an outstretched hand. Often the word, "Habari," meaning "What's the good news," is added; or "Karibu," "Welcome." It is my hope that readers will give a very friendly "Jambo" to Sungura, the hare.

ELEANOR B. HEADY

Berkeley, California
1964

1. The Scarecrow

ONCE very long ago there was a hare called Sungura, who lived by eating the villagers' crops. One day, just before harvest, he went into the field owned by Kamo and his wife, Nanira, and there he found a crop of ripe peanuts. He began digging and eating and digging some more until he had finished off almost all the nuts. Then at the edge of the clearing he saw Kamo approaching. The farmer shouted and waved his hoe, but Sungura was off immediately and disappeared into the bush.

Kamo was angry with Sungura. He went into the woods and cut a log about as big around as a child, then he nailed a piece across for arms, made a head of grass and set it up in his field to frighten the hare.

Next day Sungura returned, saw the strange thing in the peanut field, but because it looked like wood with straw on top he wasn't frightened. He ate the rest of the peanuts and went back to his home in the bush.

Kamo came to his field, and when he saw that all his peanuts had been stolen, he was angrier than ever. "I'll catch that Sungura yet," he muttered. Into the woods he went and found a tree with very sticky sap used by the villagers for glue. He collected a great mass of this sap in an earthenware pot, mixed it with red clay and returned to his field. He smeared this mixture over the scarecrow, making it look exactly like an African child, a toto.

Next day, hop-hop, out of the bush came Sungura. He went straight to the field, hoping to find a few nuts that he had overlooked. "That looks strange," he muttered. "This time I think they've put a toto to guarding the field. Guess I'll go speak to him."

Approaching the scarecrow Sungura called out, "Jambo, good morning."

The scarecrow said nothing at all.

"That's strange. He must not hear well." And

the hare came closer and shouted, "I said, good morning."

Still there was no answer. Now Sungura became a little angry. "You are real, aren't you? Answer me!" But the scarecrow was silent.

"I'll make you talk," shouted the hare, and he hit the scarecrow right in his sticky middle. When he tried to pull his foot away he was stuck fast, so he kicked with both his hind feet, and before he was finished he had all four feet stuck fast to the scarecrow. "Help," he screeched. "Help! I've been caught."

Kamo and his son, Kimondo, came running. "Ah," shouted the farmer. "So I've caught the thief at last."

"Please, good Kamo, let me go, and I'll never steal from you again," pleaded the hare.

"Absolutely not. You are going into our cooking pot." So saying he rolled Sungura in a grass mat, handed the bundle to his son, saying, "Take this thief back to the village. Give him to your mother and tell her to cook him so that we may have a good supper when I return."

"Yes, father," replied Kimondo and marched off toward the village with the bundle on his shoulder.

After he had gone a short distance, the hare began to shake the bundle. "Kimondo, listen to me, listen. What did your father ask you to do?"

The boy replied, "To take you to my mother

to cook for our supper."

"Really? I must have misunderstood."

"Why do you say that?"

"I was sure he said to cook the cock and give me a good supper. Surely since I am your guest he could do no less," said Sungura.

Kimondo was puzzled, "I'm sure I know what my father said, but . . ."

"That's just it, you aren't sure what your father said. I am. I listened."

"And just what did he say, Mr. Sungura?"

"Tell your mother to heat water for the hare to bathe, cook the cock for his dinner and put him into the skin bed to sleep."

"Well, maybe you're right," said Kimondo. "I'll do as you say."

When they arrived at the village Nanira asked, "What have you here, Kimondo?"

"Sungura, the hare, mother. Father sent him to you and said to tell you to heat water for him to bathe, kill the cock and cook it for his supper, then let him sleep in the skin bed."

"Your father said that?" Nanira shook her head doubtfully.

"I can assure you, Madam, that those were his exact words," said Sungura, poking his head from the bundle. "Please, boy, let me out of here."

Kimondo unrolled the grass mat, and the sticky hare came gleefully toward the fire. Soon Nanira had the water heated, and the hare bathed, then sat by the fire to dry his fur. Nanira went to find the cock, muttering to herself, "This seems a queer business. Imagine us entertaining Sungura."

Later, when Sungura, the hare, had eaten his fill, he was shown to the bed to sleep. This bed, like most beds in the village, was placed near a small hole which had been punched in the hut wall to provide fresh air, a hole almost the same size as a furry hare.

Just before sunset Kamo returned home from his fields calling, "Hodi, may I come in?"

Nanira answered, "Karibu, welcome, come in. How did the hoeing go?"

"It went well. Now I am very hungry."

Nanira handed him a large bowl of porridge and beans.

"But I don't want to eat beans today. I thought we would have stewed hare," said the farmer.

"So that was it?" exclaimed his wife. "I thought something strange was going on." Then she told her husband how Kimondo had told her to entertain Sungura. Kimondo, on being questioned by his father, knew that the hare had fooled him.

"And where is this clever fellow now?" asked Kamo.

"He is in the skin bed sleeping."

But when Kamo, Nanira, and Kimondo looked in the bed, Sungura had gone, leaving a bit of soft fur around the edges of the air hole.

2. The Tug of War

SUNGURA, the hare, went to the river to drink. Up from the water arose two small ears and two round eyes, watching him.

"Hello," called the hare. "Who is watching me?"

Slowly a huge creature came out of the water, shiny gray-black and very strong-looking. "It is

only I, Kiboko, the hippopotamus. I live here."

"Oh-h-h! How strong you are," marveled Sungura.

"Yes, I suppose I am strong," and Kiboko puffed with pride. "Of course, you are so small and weak that I must seem very big and strong to you."

"I'm not as weak as I look," snapped the hare.

"All the bush people know I'm strong."

"Ha, ha, what a joke!" and the great sides of the hippopotamus heaved with laughter.

Sungura was disgusted with the braggart. "We'll see," he said and hopped off into the bush.

After seventy-five hops Sungura met Tembo, the elephant, an old friend. "Jambo, Tembo, you're looking very big today."

"Always look big," rumbled the elephant.

"And strong, too," Sungura added.

"Yes, of course I'm strong. Must seem very strong to one as small and weak as you."

"I'm not so weak," said the hare. He hopped on with the elephant's laughter roaring in his ears.

Next day Sungura went into the woods and cut some long tough vines. From these he twisted a stout rope.

Returning to the river, the hare called to the hippopotamus, "Jambo, friend Kiboko. Are you feeling very strong today?"

Out of the water came the eyes, the ears, then the huge head and body. "Of course I'm feeling strong. Why do you ask?"

"You must be very strong today, for I am going to pull you out of the water with this rope."

"What?" A child like you? Pull me out of the water? That's a joke for sure." Kiboko laughed so hard that he lost his breath and sank back into the water.

After a short time, up he came. "So you think you can pull me out of the water? All right, tie the rope to my leg and let's see."

Sungura tied a very good knot to the front leg of Kiboko, then took the other end of the rope and ran into the bush. As he came through a clump of trees, he found Tembo eating leaves by the path, just where he had seen him a few minutes earlier. "Jambo, good morning, great Tembo. Are you feeling strong today?"

"Of course, I'm feeling strong, Sungura. I'm always strong."

"You must be very strong today, for I am going to pull you out of the bush with this rope."

Tembo roared with laughter. "What? You are only a child. Do you think you can pull the mighty Tembo out of the bush? I'd like to see you try." Tembo laughed until tears rolled from his tiny eyes down over his gray cheeks.

"Let me tie this rope to your leg," said the hare. "I'll run toward the river and pull from the other end."

"All right, Sungura, but I'm warning you. You just can't win."

The hare tied the end of the rope to the elephant's leg and hopped away toward the river. Tembo pulled and pulled from his place in the bush, while Kiboko pulled with all his strength from his place in the river. Neither could move the other.

As the huge animals strained and worked, Sungura hopped to the center and cut the rope, causing Kiboko to fall into the water with a great splash and Tembo to reel backwards into a very prickly thorn bush. Angrily the two arose and set out to find the hare at the other end of the rope. On the river bank they met. Kiboko stared at the rope tied to Tembo's foot.

"So," he growled, "You were pulling."

"But I thought I was pulling against Sungura," exclaimed Tembo.

"And so did I," sputtered Kiboko.

"He has fooled us both. He isn't strong, but he is very clever."

Then Kiboko returned to the river and Tembo to the trees; but Sungura, the hare, hopped away into the bush, laughing.

3. The Lion's Threats

ONCE LONG AGO when rains did not fall and there was great hunger in the land, Lingulo, the hunter, went out into the hills with his bow and arrows to look for game. He found no large animals, as most of these had died from the drought, but as the day was drawing near to sunset, he shot two hyraxes. He slung these tiny animals over his shoulder and started home.

"Well, these will give a little food and the furs will add a small warm piece to the bed covering," he muttered.

When Lingulo had come down the last hill and was starting across the plain to his village, he met Simba, the lion. He, too, was hunting, but

his sunken sides and sad expression told the hunter that he had found nothing. He bounded at the man with an angry snarl.

"I'll eat you," he growled.

Lingulo drew back, but decided to try to argue with the lion instead of running away.

"Please, Simba, do not eat me. What would my family do with no one to hunt and bring them meat? Take these hyraxes instead."

"But you are much bigger than two hyraxes," snarled the lion. "You eat the hyraxes and I'll eat you."

While they were arguing, along came Sungura, the hare.

"What is going on?" he asked.

"Simba threatens to eat me," said Lingulo.

"Why should he want to eat a thin bony thing

like you? Surely a big strong creature like Simba can find better game, perhaps a fat zebra in the hills. Why, Simba, you might as well eat a little fellow like me."

"You interfering scamp!" growled the lion. "I will eat you. I'll eat you first," and he made a dash for the hare.

But Sungura was off with a leap, dodging between bushes and shouting, "Catch me if you can."

Angrily, the lion rushed after the disappearing hare, leaving Lingulo, the hunter, free to run home; which he did.

Sungura, the hare disappeared down a fox hole, while Simba turned hungrily toward the hills.

4. The Bee Tree

SUNGURA, the hare, hopped along the forest trail, enjoying the sunshine and cool air of a bright morning. He hummed a soft tune. Then the tune turned itself into a song, "To eat honey, eat honey . . . eat honey."

Oh this is the day to eat honey,
Honey's the best thing I know.
This is the day to eat honey,
So off to get honey I go.

"How happy you sound today," said a voice from the tall grass beside the path as Kamba, the tortoise, crept slowly into sight.

"Oh, hello, Kamba. I thought I was alone."

"Not alone, but in the company of a friend," said the tortoise. "What's this about honey?"

"I'm going to get it," replied Sungura. "It's quite high up in that big mbuyu tree."

"How do you propose to get it down, my friend?"

"I've thought of that. There is a small thorn tree beside the mbuyu, a tree with many branches. I'll clumb up the small tree and into the larger one. Want to come help me?"

"Me! I can't climb!" said Kamba.

"I know that, but I could pull you up with a strong vine," offered the hare.

"That should be fun. Yes, I'll come with you. I do like honey."

"We'll need some dry grass to burn by the bees' hole so they'll come out," said Sungura as he began pulling grass beside the trail.

The hare and the tortoise, each carrying a large bundle of grass, arrived at the mbuyu tree while it was still early morning. Sungura left his grass at the foot of the tree and made his way slowly up through the prickly branches of the thorn tree. When he had crossed over to the mbuyu, he called down. "Catch hold of this vine when I drop it. Tie the grass to it and I'll pull it up. Then I'll send it back and you can come up too."

Up came the dry grass, then came Kamba, holding tightly to the vine. "Oh." he said, "How high we are! I never thought I'd be up a tree."

"Well, here you are, so let's get busy," said Sungura.

"Busy doing what?" growled a menacing voice from below.

"Simba, the lion!" shivered Sungura. "What can we do now?"

"We'll have to think of some way to make him leave," said the tortoise.

"He'll wait until we come down if it means waiting a week. We'll have to outwit him."

"You, up there. What are you doing?" snarled the lion.

"We're getting honey," answered Kamba in a frightened voice.

"Well—well, getting honey? That shouldn't take long. I'll wait for you here."

"There's no need to wait, Simba," said the hare. "We may be a very long time, and besides you may get stung by the bees. They sometimes get very angry."

"I get angry, too, especially when I'm hungry," said the lion. "You two better come down or I shall be very angry indeed."

Sungura and Kamba whispered together while Simba paced impatiently around the big mbuyu tree. "Are you coming?" he called.

"Yes, soon," answered Sungura. "Let us drop the dry grass down first."

"Very well, but hurry."

"If you don't want to get grass in your eyes, you better move away from the tree," said Kamba.

"I'll move. Send it down." Simba walked away from the foot of the tree and down came a great bundle of grass. Up out of the grass bounded Sungura, the hare, and was away into the bush before the lion realized that anything was inside the bundle "So," roared Simba in rage, "So you tricked me! Tortoise, don't you try to do the same thing. I shall stay close by the tree while you come down."

"Don't worry, I'm coming down the vine now. Don't you see me?" asked Kamba as he slid down at the feet of the lion.

"Ah! Now I have you!" growled Simba, as he took Kamba in one huge paw. He turned the tortoise over curiously and tapped his hard shell. "Now I have you, but how can I eat you with this hard sharp back you have?"

"I know a way to make the shell come off," said Kamba softly.

"You do? Tell me quickly."

"You promise you'll do as I say?"

"What can I do? I can't eat a shell," said Simba.

"Then take me to the river's edge where there is some soft mud. Rub my shell in the mud and it will soon come off."

Simba, the lion, carried Kamba to the river where he turned him upside down in the mud and began to rub him back and forth. Soon both Kamba and the lion's paw were covered with slippery mud, so slippery that the tortoise slid from the grasp of the lion and disappeared into the river.

Enraged, Simba went out into the grassland to look for bigger game.

Next morning Sungura, the hare, hopped along the forest trail, singing,

Oh, this is the day to eat honey.
Honey's the best thing I know.
This is the day to eat honey,
So off to get honey I go.

"May I come, too?" asked a voice beside the path.

"Kamba! So our plan worked."

"It worked very well, my friend."

"That honey will really taste good today," chuckled Sungura. "Come along, Kamba."

5. The Bean Pot

ONCE LONG AGO there was a great drought in
the land. Sungura, the hare, was very hungry. He decided to go to the village of the men
and ask for food. On the way he met Fisi, the
hyena.

"Jambo, Sungura, good morning," said Fisi.
"Where are you going?"

"Jambo, Fisi. I am going to the village over
in the next valley to ask for food. Things look
greener over there and I am very hungry."

"I am hungry, too. May I go with you?" asked the hyena.

"Yes, Fisi, you may come along, but please remember to be polite."

"When have I been impolite?" asked Fisi.

Sungura smiled knowingly. "Come along," he said.

When the hare and the hyena reached the village, they found that the people had little fresh food, but had stored some beans from the last crop. Karioki and his family owned a maize field near the river. "If you will cultivate the maize shamba, I will give you a pot of beans each day," said Karioki. Fisi and Sungura readily agreed, took the pot of beans and went to the field.

First they built a fire and put the beans to cook, then went to work cultivating the maize. At mid-day Sungura went to look at the beans. "Come on, Fisi," he called. "The beans are ready."

"First I must go to the stream to wash my hands," said the hyena. "Wait for me." Fisi trotted off into the bushes by the river. Once out of sight, he picked some very large banana leaves, which he wound securely around his body, fastening them with sharp thorns. Then he found two very prickly thorn branches and bound these to his head with tough vines. When he was finished he looked like a green monster with green horns.

With a blood-curdling howl, Fisi rushed out of the bush toward Sungura, who was waiting patiently beside the bean pot. What horrible creature is that? thought the hare, as he ran away in terror into the maize field.

When the hyena had frightened Sungura away, he quickly gobbled all the beans, then scurried back into the bush. Once there, he took off his disguise and walked slowly back to the bean pot. "Sungura," he called. "Where are you?"

"Here," said the hare as he came cautiously out of the maize field.

"Why didn't you stay with the beans? Someone might have stolen them."

"A terrible green monster came at me as if to eat me. He had huge thorny horns and a dreadful loud voice. Didn't you hear him?"

"I do believe you are losing your mind, Sungura. Who ever heard of such a creature?" Fisi moved toward the bean pot. "Let's eat," he said as he lifted the lid. Then the hyena gave a startled cry, "The beans are gone!"

"Gone! That monster must have stolen them," said the hare.

"Maybe," said Fisi, "But I'm of the opinion that you ate them and made up the story of the green creature."

"So you think that, do you?" Sungura was very angry. "Tomorrow we shall come again to the field. You watch carefully. You may find my story is true."

The next morning Fisi and Sungura went once more to the farmer, Karioki, were given their pot of beans and went to work hoeing maize.

At mid-day, when their beans were cooked, they stopped to eat. Once more, Fisi said, "I must go to the river to wash. Wait for me."

Fisi was gone a long time. Sungura became anxious. Finally, he called, "Fisi, hurry, I'm very hungry."

Out of the bush roared the terrible green monster. He came straight at the trembling hare, but Sungura ran only as far as the edge of the field and hid behind a large maize plant. He watched closely, as the green monster lifted the lid of the bean pot, scooped up the beans with his huge paw and ate them all. As the hyena turned to go back into the bush, the banana leaf covering his face and ears slipped to one side and Sungura knew that the green creature was Fisi. He returned to the bean pot to wait.

Fisi, the hyena, came out of the bushes. "Let us eat," he said.

"Alas, Fisi, the green monster has eaten the beans," said Sungura.

"Not again! Surely you don't expect me to believe that story again."

"I saw him, and this time I saw him eat the beans," declared the hare.

Next morning, the hare and the hyena were

given their pot of beans and went together to cultivate the maize field. At mid-day when the beans were done, Fisi said, "First I must wash," and trotted into the bush as before.

As soon as the hyena was out of sight, Sungura, the hare, lifted the lid of the bean pot and quickly ate all the beans.

Out of the bush roared the frightful green creature, but Sungura sat calmly beside the pot. Round and round ran the hyena, wailing loudly. Sungura didn't move. Finally the monster shook his thorny horns right in the face of the hare. Sungura laughed, grabbed a horn and pulled it right off the hyena's head. "Ho, ho! So it's you, Fisi? What a funny sight you are."

"So you know me?" snarled the hyena.

"Yes, and I knew you yesterday. Look into the pot."

Fisi lifted the lid, then gave a howl of disbelief. "You have eaten all the beans!"

"Yes, but you ate them all for two days, Fisi," laughed Sungura. "Remember, he who practices tricks can expect to be tricked."

6. How the Hare Learned to Swim

SUNGURA, the hare, lived near a river. On his side of the river the grass was dry, but on the opposite bank a clear stream ran into the larger channel and there were green trees and tender grass. How Sungura longed to get across that river, but the tiny hare couldn't swim. Day after day Sungura looked longingly at the other bank and wished he could find a way to get to the opposite side.

It happened that there lived nearby a large family of elephants. Sungura had frequently seen them crossing the river. They waded through with their backs high and dry above the water. How he envied them. I only wish I were as big as an elephant, thought the hare. Then on second thought, he wondered if that would be so nice after all. Elephants couldn't curl up and sleep comfortably in a cool hollow under a log, nor could they hide in the tall grass.

One day the elephants came down to the river bank very close to Sungura's burrow. He watched

them closely as they lumbered toward the water swinging their snaky long noses in front of them. Then he had an idea. Cautiously he approached the largest of the beasts, who was carrying a leather bag on his back and asked politely, "Oh, great Tembo, king of the bushland, would you be so kind as to do a favor for a humble creature like me?"

The elephant, startled to be addressed by someone so far below on the ground, looked with his tiny nearsighted eyes for the speaker. "Oh, it's you, Sungura," he said, "and what would you like?"

"Please, most honored Tembo, I should like a ride on your back to the other side of the river."

"Is that all? I see no reason why that can't be arranged. Come over here and sit on my trunk and I will hoist you up beside my bag of honey." The elephant swung his trunk down so that the hare could climb into the curve he made at the end and with a swish he swung it around and put Sungura down on his broad back beside the honey.

"Oh," gasped the hare, "what a wonderful ride."

"Now sit quietly, my friend, and you shall have another ride even more wonderful." Tembo stepped into the water, followed by his family. Sungura in delight sat securely on top.

When they were out into the water, Sungura looked closely at the honey bag, sticky on the outside. The hare licked a few drops from the outside—"Mmmmm—good," he whispered. Then he carefully opened the top of the bag and took just a little lick, then a little more and a little more, until he had eaten every bit of the honey! He dropped a little on Tembo's back. "What do I feel?" asked the elephant.

"Only tears of joy and gratitude, most honored Tembo, my tears because I am so happy," answered Sungura.

"Only too glad to help," said Tembo as he splashed on across the stream.

Just as they reached the opposite bank Sungura said to the elephant, "Oh, kind sir, there are many large birds here. I am afraid of them. Will you please give me some stones to throw so that I may frighten them away."

The obliging Tembo picked up some small stones with his trunk and handed them up. "There you are. Those should be just right."

"Thank you, great Tembo. You are very kind."

Sungura threw only a few of the stones. The rest he put into the honey bag. Then he asked to be set down.

Swish, he rode the elephant's trunk to the ground and scurried away into the grass.

Tembo and his family went on down the trail to their meadow. When the big elephant reached up and brought down the honey bag from his back, he was startled to find that the honey had turned to lumps. Then he opened the bag and found stones—nothing but stones! He cried out in anger and when the other elephants came to see what was wrong he said, "That ungrateful hare! Look what he did after I had befriended him. He left me stones for my honey."

Many days later when Sungura was happily eating some new shoots of tender grass at the water's edge, Tembo came swaying silently out of the woods. The hare didn't see him until he spoke. "Good day, Sungura, and how do you like your new home?"

Startled, the hare replied, "Oh, kind sir, I—I—I." His voice trailed off into nothing.

"Perhaps you'd like another ride on my back," suggested Tembo.

Sungura was puzzled by the generosity of the big elephant, but the tantalizing prospect of another ride overcame his desire to run away. "Oh, yes sir, if you'd be so kind, sir," he said.

With a great flourish Tembo swung his trunk to the ground and picked up the hare. With a tremendous swish, the elephant swung Sungura around and threw him—splash—far out into the river. Down went the hare—up he came sputtering and gasping, "Help—help—I can't swim."

"Time you learned," said the elephant with a chuckle.

Round and round bobbed Sungura, struggling and kicking and finally swimming uncertainly to the bank. Out he crawled, wet and shaking.

In the distance he heard the rumbling laugh of Tembo. "Next time you try to trick me, remember I have a good memory."

Sungura learned more than gratitude from his thorough ducking in the river. He learned how to swim.

7. The Wonderful Tree

ONCE VERY LONG ago there was a great drought. No rain fell for many months. The grass became brown and dry. Fruits and berries withered and dropped to the ground. All the wild creatures were hungry. Simba, the lion, called the animals together for a big baraza or meeting.

"All you who dwell in the bush and veld," he

said, "we are starving. Does anyone know where we might find food?"

There was silence. The animals shook their heads sadly.

Through the grass hopped Sungura, the hare. "Sorry to be late," he said. "Have you decided what we shall do to find food?"

"No," said the lion sadly. "Have you any suggestions?"

"Well," said Sungura, "it may not be true, but I have heard that Koko, the wise old woman with the crooked back, owns a wonderful tree full of delicious fruit. It is a very tall tree and the fruit cannot be reached. Koko alone knows the secret that will make the fruit loosen its hold on the branches and fall to the ground."

"Perhaps Koko would show us the tree," suggested Suguya, the dik-dik.

"That won't help," said Sungura. "We must also learn the secret that makes the fruit fall."

"Let us send some of the animals to Koko and ask her to give us her magic secret," said Ngiri, the wart hog.

"Yes, yes," shouted the animals. "Send someone soon!"

"Wise words, Ngiri," said the lion as he looked over the group. "I'll appoint Sungura, the hare, because he is a fast runner and clever; Kiboko, the hippopotamus, because he is large; and Kamba, the tortoise, because he is patient."

"Yes, yes," agreed the animals.

So Sungura, Kiboko and Kamba set off to the village to find the owner of the wonderful tree. When they reached her hut, the hare called out, "Hodi, Koko, may we come in? We'd like to talk to you."

A very old woman, dark and bent like a charred stick, put her head out the doorway.

"What do you want of me?" she asked.

"Koko," said Sungura with a bow, "we have heard of your magic tree and have come to ask that you give us some of the fruit. Because there has been no rain, the animals are starving."

"The tree yields its fruit for those who know the magic word," said Koko. "I alone know it."

"Will you please tell us your secret?" pleaded Kiboko, the hippopotamus.

The old woman hobbled closer, peering intently at the three. "You do look hungry," she said. "I don't need all the fruit for myself. If you can remember my instructions you can cause the fruit to fall to earth."

"Do tell us quickly," urged Sungura.

"Yes, do," rumbled Kiboko.

"Tell us slowly and carefully," said Kamba, the tortoise.

"Very well, now listen, all of you. The tree that bears fruit for all to eat is over seven hills, through seven valleys, beside a spring that runs a few drops of water even when there has been no rain.

When you get to the tree stand beneath it and repeat the magic word slowly three times. When this is done properly, the fruit will fall to the ground."

"That is all very well," said the hare. "But you haven't told us the magic word."

"Patience, you shall know it soon. I can tell the word to only one living soul at a time. Choose one of your number and I shall whisper the word in his ear."

"You should be the one to go to find the tree, Sungura," suggested Kiboko. "You can run very fast and would be there before Kamba or I could get started."

"Yes, Sungura, you must go," agreed Kamba, the tortoise.

Sungura, the hare, stepped forward and Koko whispered the word in his ear. He was off in a flash, hurrying over one hill, through one valley and on and on as fast as he could hop. On the top of the sixth hill Sungura tried to leap over a very large bush. His feet caught in the top branches and he fell down into the prickly center, kicking and squirming. He struggled from the bush and started on. Suddenly he stopped, muttering to himself. "The secret word! I can't remember the secret word!" Sadly, the hare returned to the hut of the old woman.

"Did the fruit fall?" asked Kamba, the tortoise.

"I was caught in a bush and forgot the secret

word," admitted Sungura sadly.

"You forgot the word?" exclaimed Kiboko. "Let me go. I'm sure I'll remember it."

So Koko whispered the magic word to the hippopotamus and away he waddled to find the wonderful tree. When Kiboko reached the bottom of the sixth valley, he came to a very large log blocking the path. He tried to step over it, stumbled and fell on his head into the dust. He struggled to his feet, shook the dust from his thick skin and started on.

"Oh, how terrible!" Kiboko stopped still. "I've forgotten the secret word!" He stood very quietly, trying one word after another, "Mbala, Kilaka, Kitoto." Finally he shook his head in dismay. "I just can't remember the word." Sadly he returned to the hut of the old woman.

"Did the fruit fall?" asked Kamba eagerly when the hippopotamus came in sight.

"I fell over a log and forgot the secret word," admitted Kiboko with tears in his eyes.

"Then Kamba, the tortoise, must go," said the woman. She whispered the secret word to the tortoise and he began his journey to find the wonderful tree. He went very slowly. When he had climbed the first hill, he stopped and repeated the secret word, "Mbilaka," slowly and carefully. At the bottom of each valley, he repeated it. When, after a very long time, he saw a high spreading tree, he began to think with every creeping step,

"Mbilaka, Mbilaka, Mbilaka."

Kamba gazed upward at the branches, far above the ground. The tree was so high and so wide that it shut out his whole view of the sky. What a wonderful sight! Every branch was drooping with heavy red fruit. Slowly the tortoise circled the tree, repeating, "Mbilaka, Mbilaka, Mbilaka." Down came the fruit, like heavy red rain. Kamba could hardly believe his eyes.

"What are you doing?" twittered a voice from the treetop.

Kamba looked up to see Manari, the green parakeet, surrounded by his huge family.

"Jambo, hello, Manari. I'm getting fruit to feed the animals. They are all hungry."

"But where are the others?" asked the parakeet.

"Alas, away in the bush and veld. I fear it will take a long time to find them. I had forgotten about that when I caused the fruit to fall."

"Don't worry," chirped Manari. "My family flies fast. We will call the animals to the feast." So the green parakeets flew away across the bushland, bobbing their bright red heads and calling, "Come to the wonderful tree. Kamba has food for you. Follow us!"

From all directions came the bush folk. Sungura, the hare, and Kiboko, the hippopotamus, arrived last of all.

"So you remembered the word," marveled the hare.

"How did you do it?" asked Kiboko.

"Slowly and carefully," replied Kamba, the tortoise, as he began nibbling the delicious red fruit from the wonderful tree.

8. The Baboon and the Hare

Long, long ago, Gudo, the baboon, lived with men and was like one of them. The chief of Gudo's village had a beautiful daughter called Nanura. The baboon loved her very much and asked her father if he might marry her.

"You may have Nanura for your wife if you will bring me a gift of three young hares," said the chief.

"Very well. I shall return with them soon. Prepare the wedding feast," said Gudo as he took up his knapsack and bounded away into the forest.

Sungura, the hare, and his wife had a cozy burrow at the foot of a wild fig tree, and in this burrow lived their three fat children. On this day, Sungura and his wife had left the children in the burrow while they went out, each in a different direction, to look for food.

Gudo, the baboon, came through the forest, sniffing under logs and behind bushes. He found those fat furry hares, popped them into his knapsack and started back toward the village. "What a lovely gift these will make," he muttered. "My father-in-law to be will be very pleased." But the young hares were heavy, and Gudo became tired. He walked slower and slower, finally sitting down on a stone to rest.

As the baboon sat thinking of how happy he

would be with the beautiful Nanura, Sungura, the hare, came along.

"Jambo, good morning, Gudo," he said. "You look very happy."

"Indeed, I am happy, Sungura. Today is my wedding day and I am on my way to the wedding feast. I am taking my father-in-law this gift of ripe plums. The knapsack grew heavy, so I stopped to rest."

"Congratulations, Gudo. It isn't everyone who has a wedding feast prepared for him. You must have a generous father-in-law."

"Oh, yes indeed," agreed Gudo. "And because he is so generous I must hurry with my gift for him. But it is very heavy and I'm tired."

"Would you like some help?" offered Sungura. "I could carry the knapsack to the village while you hurry on so you won't miss any of the fun."

"Oh, how kind of you, Sungura. Such thoughtfulness!" and the baboon handed the knapsack to the hare and bounded away to the village.

Sungura carried the heavy bag along the path. "These plums must be very juicy," he said to himself. "They are certainly heavy."

Above him in the treetops he heard a tiny urgent voice, "Hon-e-e-e, follow me-e-e-e." It was Orushigo, the honey bird. "Follow me-e-e-e," twittered the bird. "Honey, Hon-e-e-e-e-ee."

Forgetting about the weight of the knapsack, Sungura followed the little bird. Orushigo was never wrong. He always knew where the bees hid their honey.

"Follow me-e-e-ee," called the bird.

"I'm coming," shouted Sungura as he scrambled through the bush with the knapsack.

In the top of a big old, half dead tree Orushigo stopped. "Here, se-e-e-e-ee," he called.

"Thank you, thank you. Now I can get the honey," said the hare.

He put down the knapsack with a thump. "Ow!" screeched a small voice.

"What was that?"

"Us, father. Let us out. We'd like some honey, too."

"That sounds like the voices of my children," marveled Sungura.

"Yes, yes, let us out of this stuffy old sack where that wicked Gudo put us."

Quickly the hare untied the cord that held the top of the bag and out rolled his three furry babies.

"Whee! we're out of that dark place," They shouted. "Now for some honey!"

From a hole near the foot of the tree, came a stream of bees, angry and ready to fight. Sungura grabbed up the knapsack, put the open top firmly over the bees' hole so that the bees flew out into the bag. When he had a sack full, he quickly drew the cord so that none of them could escape. Then, with all the bees safely out of the way he reached into the tree and brought out a sticky dripping honey comb. This he divided into five pieces, giving one to each of the children, eating one himself and keeping one to take to his wife.

"Now," said the hare when they had eaten, "You children run home. Take this honey to your mother. I shall go on to the wedding feast of Gudo, the baboon." Sungura took up the knapsack and turned toward the village.

There was great activity in the open place between the huts, while in front of every house burned a fire over which hung roasting meat or a boiling pot. In the center sat the chief and his family on a platform decorated with green branches.

Gudo, the baboon, was waiting at the edge of the clearing. When he saw the hare coming, he looked very pleased. "You've finally come. What kept you?"

"Orushigo, the honey bird, led me to a bee tree. I can't resist honey," and Sungura smacked his lips.

"Quick, give me the knapsack. My father-in-law is impatient for his gift." Gudo snatched the bag and hurried to the chief. "Look in the bag and you'll find just what you want most," urged the baboon.

The old man took the bag, untied the cord and out roared a cloud of angry bees, stinging the chief cruelly. "So," he shouted. "This is the kind of son-in-law you'd be, playing tricks on me. There will be no wedding. Because you have deceived me, you may no longer live in the village, but must find a home in the bush. All my people will despise your name."

At the edge of the clearing, Sungura chuckled to himself, "Deceit begs to be deceived," and hopped away to his burrow.

9. Son of the Long One

SUNGURA, the hare, was out in his garden all morning. When he returned to his house under the roots of a big thorn tree, he saw some very strange-looking tracks in the dust of his doorway, long tracks, as if some huge animal had gone in. Sungura was frightened. He had never seen such tracks and was quite convinced that some monster was inside his house. He called out in a

shaky voice, "Hodi, who is inside my house?"

A big voice replied, "I am the warrior son of the long one whose anklets became unfastened in a great battle and are dragging behind. I can crush the mighty rhinoceros to earth and the elephant trembles at my voice. Beware of me!"

Sungura was indeed frightened. What sort of monster is in my house? he thought. He shuddered at the thought of any creature whose anklets dragging could make these tracks. He must be huge and much too strong to be chased away by a hare. Sungura decided to get help from some of his friends and started off into the bush. He had gone only a few feet when he met the jackal, Mbweha. "Oh, clever Mbweha," he cried, "Please help me. Some strange, strong animal is in my house and refuses to come out. Perhaps you who are so cunning can get him to go away."

"Well, I'll talk to this mysterious intruder, but I'm not sure he'll listen."

Sungura and Mbweha approached the door of the house. "See the tracks," said the hare. "Aren't they strange?"

"They are indeed," agreed the jackal. Then he called out, "Hodi, who is in the house of my friend, Sungura?"

Again the big voice answered, "I am the warrior son of the long one whose anklets became unfastened in a great battle and are dragging behind. I can crush the mighty rhinoceros to earth and the elephant trembles at my voice. Beware of me!"

Now Mbweha was as frightened as his friend. "He sounds very ferocious, Sungura. I think we better go away and leave him." So the hare and the jackal trotted into the bush, but Sungura was still determined to get the intruder out of his house.

Next they met a leopard. "Oh, Chui, my friend, I need your help," said Sungura. "Someone very strong is inside my house and refuses to come out."

"Refuses? It's your house, isn't it?"

"Of course, Chui, but he seems to think no one is strong enough to make him leave and now I have no place to sleep tonight. What shall I do?"

"I'll go have a talk with this fellow," said Chui. "Perhaps my reputation for cunning has come to his ears. He will probably go away when I arrive."

The three friends trotted back to the house of the hare and this time, Chui, the leopard, called out, "Who is in the house of my friend, Sungura?"

For a moment there was no answer, then just as before came this reply, "I am the warrior son of the long one whose anklets became unfastened in a great battle and are dragging behind. I can crush the mighty rhinoceros to earth. The elephant trembles at the sound of my voice. Beware of me!"

"What could one as strong as I do against him? He can crush the rhinoceros. I think we better go away and leave him," said Chui. "I have never met such a creature and I have no desire to do so."

"But he has my house," wailed Sungura.

"You'll just have to find another." said Mbweha.

"Of course, you'd be foolish to try to fight with the son of the long one," agreed Chui.

With that the jackal and the leopard ran into the bush, leaving the disappointed hare looking sadly at his house.

Sungura started out again, not quite sure where he was going. Find another house, indeed! That wasn't as easily done as some people seemed to suppose. Then he heard a booming voice above him, "Is that you way down there, Sungura? Thought you usually took a nap in the afternoon. Something wrong?"

Sungura looked up at the huge swaying trunk of Tembo, the elephant. "Something is very wrong, Tembo," he said. "Come with me and I'll show you."

As they walked toward the hare's home, Sungura told the elephant of the intruder and how he refused to leave. "I think I can make him go," said Tembo. "I am the largest animal in the bush. Surely he will be afraid of me."

When they reached the hare's tree Tembo called out, "Hodi, may I come in, you who have taken the house of my friend, Sungura. I am Tembo, king of the bush."

"Ha, ha, ha," laughed the big voice, "Come in

indeed!'' Don't you know that you are much too large to come in? Besides, I am stronger than you. I am the warrior son of the long one whose anklets became unfastened in a great battle and are dragging behind. I can crush the mighty rhinoceros to earth and you, Tembo, should tremble at my voice for I am very mighty.''

"I have never heard of such a creature," said Tembo shakily. "Perhaps you will have to let him stay in your house, Sungura. I wouldn't dare try to get him out. He is much too strong for me."

"Well thank you, Tembo," said the hare. "I guess there is no one to help." Sungura hopped sadly off into the bush and sat down on a round stone to think. A huge tear rolled down each cheek. "My lovely home," he sobbed. "How shall I ever find another?"

Just then there was a stirring in the grass and a small rasping voice asked, "What is the trouble? Perhaps I can help."

Sungura looked down into the funny ugly face of Chura, the frog. "Oh, my small friend, you cannot help. Some very strong creature is in my house and will not go away. Mbweha, Chui, and Tembo have all tried to get him to leave, but he refuses. He sounds so terrible. What shall I do?" Sungura began to cry harder.

"There, there, Sungura," croaked the frog. "Don't be so upset. There must be a way to get rid of this house-stealer. He can't be so very large, or he couldn't get into your house."

"True, I didn't think of that," said Sungura.

"Now let's go to your house and I'll see what I can do."

Sungura arose doubtfully and the two friends hopped back to the hole under the tree. The frog looked carefully at the strange tracks and then winked at his friend, calling out in a loud voice, "Who is in the house of my friend, Sungura?"

Once again the intruder replied, "I am the warrior son of the long one whose anklets became unfastened in a great battle. I can crush the mighty rhinoceros to earth and the elephant trembles at the sound of my voice. Beware of me!"

And Chura replied, "I am strong and a leaper. If you lon't leave the house of my friend I shall leap upon you and off again before you can harm me. You will not like my leaping."

The voice that came from the hare's house was a much smaller one this time, a voice that sounded frightened. "Please, oh leaper, I am only Nyodu, the caterpillar. I shall come out if you promise not to harm me."

Sungura could hardly believe his eyes when the tiny furry creature crawled slowly out of his house. "And to think all of us were afraid of you —all but Chura, who is very brave."

"Not brave at all," laughed the frog. "I have learned never to believe a thief. If you'll remember that you will save yourself a lot of trouble."

10. Trust Your Friends

INTINI, THE OTTER, and Mantswane, the badger, were friends. Intini was a splendid fisherman, often catching more fish than his children could eat. When there were too many fish for the otters, Intini always took the extras as a gift to the home of his friend, Mantswane, the badger.

Mantswane loved honey. He was very skillful at finding bees' nests in the woods and often found more than his children could eat. Whenever this happened, the badger took the extra honey and gave it to his friend, Intini, the otter.

Sungura, the hare, lived in a hole beneath a

huge thorn tree in the bush. Many times he had seen the otter and the badger pass by together, laughing and talking gaily. Wonder what they do here, he thought. Guess I'll watch them and find out. So one day when the friends came by, Sungura crept stealthily from his burrow and followed. He saw Intini, the otter, take two beautiful fish from his knapsack and give them to the badger. Then Mantswane took a gourd full of honey from his sack and gave it to Intini.

"Well, well," marveled Sungura. "So they have so much to eat that they give some away!"

Next day at the same hour the hare watched closely. From one side of the bush came the otter, from the other the badger. When they met, they seemed delighted.

"Good morning, friend Intini," called the badger. "I found a really fine bee tree today, enough for a feast for all of us," and he handed a huge gourd sticky with honey to the otter.

"Thank you, friend Mantswane," replied Intini. "I have been lucky, too. The fish were big and lazy. I caught enough for all," and he handed the badger three beautiful shining fish.

From his place in the bushes, Sungura, the hare, thought greedily of what a lovely feast the badger and the otters would have that day.

Some days later, Sungura from his burrow heard someone approaching. He peeked out to see Intini, the otter, coming. He carried a knapsack and from its top protruded the shining tail of a large fish. Sungura stepped out. "Good morning, Intini. Art you starting on a long journey?"

"Oh, good morning, Sungura," said the otter gaily. "I'm only coming here to meet my friend Mantswane, the badger. I have a nice fish for him."

Sungura looked solemn. Shaking his head dolefully he said, "I don't think you should give it to him."

"And why not, I ask you? I always give Mantswane my extra fish and he gives me honey."

"He doesn't want any more of your fish, Intini. The last you gave him made his children ill. They choked on the bones. He is very angry with you. If you take my advice you'll not wait for him, but go home now."

"If what you say is true," said the otter, "I shall return home now."

"It's true, all right," declared Sungura. "Hurry before he comes."

"But what shall I do with this lovely fish?"

Sungura shook his head solemnly. "It would be a shame to carry it home again. Now it happens that I like fish. Perhaps I could take it off your hands."

"Of course, take it if you can use it." Intini, the otter, took the fish from the knapsack, dropped it at the feet of the hare and hurried off to his home in the river as fast as his short legs could go.

Chuckling, Sungura carried the fish to his bur-

row and returned to the path to wait for Mantswane, the badger.

Mantswane appeared soon, shuffling the dry
leaves as he came through the bush. Out stepped
Sungura.

"Good morning, friend Mantswane. A nice day
for traveling."

"Good morning to you, Sungura. You are
wrong. I'm not traveling."

"Not traveling? But I thought you must be
going on a long journey from the size of that
gourd you're carrying."

"This?" laughed Mantswane. "Why, this is only
honey to give to my friend Intini, the otter. He
and his children love honey."

Sungura looked serious. "Are you sure of that?
Only today I saw Intini in the bush and he told
me how your honey made all his childen very ill.
He is angry with you about it."

"Really? How dreadful! I thought he was my
friend."

"He was, but is really angry with you now,"
said the hare.

"What should I do?" asked the badger.

"If I were you, I'd not wait for the otter, but
go straight home before he comes."

"I'll do that. I don't want to carry this heavy
gourd back to my hole. What can I do with it?"

"It just happens that I like honey. Perhaps I
could relieve you of the burden," and Sungura

looked very solemn.

"Splendid. It's yours." The badger put his heavy gourd at the feet of the hare and trotted away to his home in the bush.

Several days passed and neither Intini, the otter, nor Mantswane, the badger, went into the woods. One day, Mantswane was hunting for bees' nests in tall trees near the river when he came face to face with Intini.

"Oh, it's you," he said crossly.

"Yes, Mantswane, and are you still angry with me?"

"But I thought you were angry with me. Sungura said—"

"Sungura! So that's it," exclaimed the otter. "I fear he's deceived us both. He told me my fish made your children sick."

"And he told me my honey made your children sick," added the badger.

"Why did we believe him? He tricked us both," said Intini.

"It is better to trust a friend than to believe an outsider," said Mantswane, the badger, with a sigh.

11. The Talking House

ONCE LONG AGO Simba, the lion, went hunting. He was very hungry because he had found no game for many days.

Sungura, the hare, was out for a morning stroll, when there in the path ahead of him appeared the lion, looking very cross.

"Jambo, good morning," said Sungura politely.

Simba stared at the small furry hare. "You're certainly not big," he said, "But I'll eat you anyway."

Sungura gave one frightened hop and disappeared into the bush.

"So," snarled the lion, "You think I can't catch you?" He bounded through the thicket after the hare, but Sungura hid beneath the roots of a tree and Simba didn't find him, although he scratched himself cruelly on the thorns as he searched.

Next morning Simba, in an angry mood, went looking for the hare again. He met Kamba, the tortoise. "Good morning, Kamba. Could you tell me where Sungura, the hare, makes his home?"

I should like to visit him."   ,

"You? Visit Sungura?" asked the tortoise in amazement.

"Yes," replied Simba. "Tell me where he lives."

"That is very difficult, for Sungura seldom sleeps in the same house twice."

"Really?"

"Yes, indeed. You'll have to find him for yourself." Kamba, the tortoise, crept into the tall grass.

Now it happened that the hare and the tortoise were good friends. Kamba went directly to the house of Sungura. "Hodi," he called, "May I come in?"

"Karibu, welcome, friend tortoise," said the hare.

"I have come to warn you, Sungura. Simba, the lion, is searching for you. He asked me to tell him where you live. I said you moved from house to house."

"Why did you say that, Kamba?"

"So he wouldn't know where to look for you," replied the tortoise.

"That was clever, but he'll ask someone else. Simba doesn't give up that easily."

"What will you do?" asked Kamba.

"I shall move immediately. When he finds my house, I won't be in it."

So Sungura, the hare, moved his family to another house under the root of a huge mbuyu tree. When they were comfortably settled, he returned and hid in the bushes near his old grass house beside a thorn bush.

Simba, the lion, did exactly as Sungura had predicted. He asked every small animal he met to show him the home of Sungura. All refused, until he met Nungu, the porcupine, who was known for his stupidity.

"Good morning, Nungu" said Simba. "Can you tell me the way to the home of Sungura, the hare?"

"He lives in the first grass house over the next hill," said Nungu, "right next to that big thorn bush."

"Thank you! You are a very clever creature," and Simba was off over the hill with a bound.

Simba, the lion, found Sungura's house. "Hodi," he called. "Let me come in." There was no answer. "Hodi," he shouted. "I know you live here, Sungura. Let me in!" Still there was silence. Simba cautiously put his head through the doorway. The house was empty! He crept inside and curled up to wait for the return of the hare.

All this time Sungura had been watching from a hiding place in the bush nearby. When the lion was well hidden, the hare came out and pretended to be coming home down the trail. He approached his house, bowed politely, and said in a very courteous voice, "Salaam, house; greetings, house."

Simba, the lion, was puzzled. He had never heard of a house that could talk.

Then in a loud voice the hare said, "This is

strange. Perhaps the house has a stomach ache. Every day when I pass this house, I call 'Salaam' and the house answers me. But today someone must be in the house, for the friendly house is afraid to speak."

Then the lion replied cautiously, "Salaam."

"O! Ho!" laughed Sungura. "So it's you, Simba? And did you ever know a house that could talk?" With a great leap Sungura sped away into the bush.

12. Wanja's Choice

ONCE UPON A TIME long ago, Sungura, the hare, went out to seek a wife. At the home of his old uncle, he met Wanja, a beautiful hare maiden, and promptly fell in love with her. He asked her to marry him and she replied, "Sungura, you are the only one for me."

The hare built a beautiful grass house for Wanja. When it was finished he said, "Now I shall

go out and get food so that we may have a great
wedding feast. Wait for me here."

Wanja made the house tidy and awaited the
return of Sungura. Soon there was a shouting at
the door, "Hodi, may I come in?"

Wanja looked out to see Tembo, the elephant.
"Go away," said the hare maiden.

"Why do you say that?" asked Tembo.

"I have no food for you."

"But I don't want food. I want to talk to you."

"What would you say?" asked Wanja.

"I'd like to marry you."

Then Wanja replied, "My answer is, no. I shall marry only Sungura, for whom I am waiting."

Sadly Tembo went away toward the forest. On the way he met Simba, the lion, and said to him. "I have been to ask the beautiful Wanja to marry me. She refused. Why don't you go? You are so handsome that she would never refuse you."

Simba, the lion, came to the door of the little grass house, "Hodi, may I come in?" he called.

Wanja looked out and when she saw the lion said, "Go away."

"Why do you say that?" asked Simba.

"I have no food for you."

"But I don't want food. I want to talk to you," said the lion.

"What would you say?"

"I'd like to marry you."

Then Wanja replied, "My answer is, no. I shall marry only Sungura, for whom I am waiting."

Then Simba went away into the bush where he met Nyumbu, the wildebeeste. "Good day Nyumbu," he said. "I have been to ask Wanja, the beautiful hare maiden, to be my wife. She refused. Why don't you go? You have such a lovely white beard and pretty tail. Surely she will not refuse you."

So Nyumbu, the wildebeeste, went to the little grass house. "Hodi," he called. "May I come in?"

Wanja looked out and saw the wildebeeste.

"Go away," she said.

"Why do you say that?" asked Nyumbu.

"I have no food for you."

"But I don't want food. I want to talk to you," said the wildebeeste.

"What would you say?"

"I'd like to marry you."

Then Wanja replied, "My answer is, no. I shall marry only Sungura, for whom I am waiting."

Sadly Nyumbu went away into the bush, where he met Pofu, the eland. "Good day, Pofu," said Nyumbu. "I have been to ask Wanja, the beautiful hare maiden, to be my wife. She refused. Why don't you go? You are so majestic and have such handsome horns, surely she will not refuse you."

So Pofu, the eland, went to the little grass house. "Hodi," he called. "May I come in?"

"Go away," said Wanja.

"Why do you say that?" asked Pofu.

"I have no food for you."

"But I don't want food. I want to talk to you," said the eland.

"What would you say?"

"I'd like to marry you."

Then Wanja replied, "My answer is, no. I shall marry only Sungura, for whom I am waiting."

Then Pofu went sadly away into the bush where he met Punda Malia, the zebra. "Jambo, Good day, Punda Malia," he said. "I have been to ask Wanja, the beautiful hare maiden, to be my wife.

She refused. Why don't you go? You are so beautiful with your black and white stripes, that she surely will not refuse you."

So Punda Malia, the zebra, went to the little grass house. "Hodi," he called, "may I come in?"

Wanja looked out and when she saw the zebra she said, "Go away."

"Why do you say that?" asked the zebra.

"I have no food for you."

"But I don't want food. I want to talk to you, to ask you to marry me," said Punda Malia.

Then Wanja replied, "My answer is, no. I shall marry only Sungura, for whom I am waiting."

So Punda Malia went sadly into the bush to tell the other animals that he, too, had been refused by the beautiful hare maiden.

Sungura, the hare, returned to the little grass house bringing food for the wedding feast. When everything was ready he went out into the bush and invited all the other animals to the celebration. While they were eating, the animals marveled that Wanja should choose Sungura, who was so small and not handsome.

"Will you tell us, beautiful maiden, why you chose Sungura for a husband?" asked Simba, the lion.

"I will tell you," said Wanja. "He is small, but so am I. He has long ears; so have I. He has gray fur; so have I. We are always happiest with our own kind."

13. The Ostrich Chicks

Esida, the ostrich, had a wonderful nest of eggs, twelve of them. For many days she sat patiently on the eggs, she and her husband, Mbuni; for like all good ostrich couples they took turns at everything connected with raising a family. Finally the eggs began to hatch. One by one they cracked until twelve fuzzy chicks came out of the white shells, chicks whose gray-brown color was much like that of the earth. As soon as the chicks were dry the proud ostrich parents took their new family out to show them off to the other animals.

"What beautiful children you have," said Sungura, the hare.

"They are indeed," agreed Esida.

"See what lovely long necks they have," added Mbuni.

"Yes, their necks are long—but lovely? Well—maybe," said the hare, who was not too fond of long necks.

For many days the ostrich family grazed quietly by day and returned to the shelter of their nest in the tall grass by night. It became more and more difficult to keep track of the children. One evening when the family was returning to the nest the young chicks decided to have a game and raced off across the plains far ahead of their parents. Esida called frantically for them to return at once. Mbuni flapped his huge wings and cried, "Come back, come back at once." But they were having too much fun. On they raced.

Now Simba, the lion, had been watching from a clump of brush. What a wonderful dinner those chicks would make, he thought. And so many of them too, enough for more than one meal. Slowly he crept upon them and bounded silently into their midst. The startled chicks scattered, squawking wildly, but clever Simba talked to them softly, "Don't be afraid, my children. I only want to take you and show you the wonderful cave where I live. Wouldn't you like to see it? It's much cozier than your home in the grass."

"We would like to see it," said one chick. "Take us now before our parents arrive to spoil the fun."

So before the frantic Esida and Mbuni could reach them, Simba had driven the ostrich chicks over a hill and out of sight. I'll not eat them now, he thought. I'll save them for some time when I'm hungrier. He took them to his cave and when he had them inside, he rolled a huge stone across the entrance so they couldn't escape.

Now the chicks were really frightened. They pleaded with Simba to let them go back to their own home, but he had no idea of doing that. "Ha, ha!" he laughed. "You're my chicks now."

Esida and Mbuni were frantic with fear for their children. It was well known that Simba was the most hated animal in the bushland. Who would be brave enough to help them against this thief?

They went to Sungura, who was usually very wise. "Oh, Sungura," pleaded Mbuni, "Please ask Simba to return our children."

Sungura was afraid of Simba, and although he felt sorry for the ostriches, he knew he could do nothing against the cunning lion. "I'm sorry, my friends, but Simba is much too strong. He wouldn't listen to me."

Next they asked Nguruwe, the wart hog, for help. "If the lion has your children, then they are his. Don't you know that no one can get them away from him?"

Sadly the ostrich parents moved from one group of animals to the next. The answer was always the same. Everyone was afraid of Simba and would do nothing to help them. Finally they came to the burrow of Garibobo, the mongoose.

"Please, Garibobo," pleaded Esida, "you are so clever that surely you can think of some way to make Simba return our children."

The mongoose felt sorry indeed for Mbuni and Esida, who were great favorites among the bush folk. After several moments of deep thought and much wrinkling of his furry brows, he said, "Yes, I have a plan that may work. Anyway, let us try it. We shall call a meeting of all the animals, tell them that something very important is afoot. Surely Simba with his great curiosity will be unable to stay away. If he comes to the meeting I'm sure we can get your children back. Now do exactly as I say."

"We'll do anything, oh wise Garibobo, anything to get our children back." said Esida.

"Very well. I'll call the meeting for tomorrow morning beside the large ant hill near Simba's cave."

Garibobo, the mongoose, began at once to inform the animals. He bounded across the grassland, loopity, loopity, shouting for all to hear, "Big meeting, verrrry important. Everyone must come. We'll gather when the sun throws our shadows around us. Everyone remember. Come to the tall ant hill beside Simba's cave."

The animals listened and when the sun stood in the center of the sky, they assembled at the ant hill. Last of all came Simba, and to show his complete contempt for the ostriches, he had the chicks with him. He took great care to keep them far from their parents in a little group at one side. Mbuni and Esida told how Simba had taken their children, while the villain sat grinning wickedly. Each animal in turn was asked by Mbuni, "Are these chicks not ours? Won't you help us make Simba return them?"

The animals were so afraid of Simba that they couldn't answer truthfully and each timidly declared that the chicks must remain with Simba. Even Sungura was afraid to declare his belief that the ostriches should have their own children. "I guess they belong to Simba," he said sadly.

Last of all Mbuni asked Garibobo, "Oh wise mongoose, do you not think that Simba should return our children?"

"What would a tiny one like him know about it?" snarled the lion.

Garibobo looked slowly around the circle of animals to make sure that all were listening. Last of all he looked at the lion, then edging closer to the ant hill, he said, "Of course the chicks belong to the ostriches. Who ever saw a lion's children with feathers?"

With a snarl of rage, Simba made a leap for the mongoose. Garibobo dived down the hole in the ant hill. Simba sat at the hole and growled, "I'll wait right here until you come out. Don't think you can get away!"

While Simba was waiting to catch the mongoose, Esida and Mbuni quietly gathered their chicks and made off into the bush. In a towering rage, Simba waited for Garibobo at the hole in the ant hill. Then away off on a distant knoll he heard a laugh and a shout, "Here I am, Simba. I went out through a hole on the other side of the ant hill. You were too busy watching the entrance to see me."

The lion gave a great roar of rage, a roar that made the grass quiver all the way to the distant hills.

"Remember, Simba," called Garibobo. "He who practices treachery is asking to be tricked."

14. The Greedy Hyena

ONE DAY FISI, the hyena, hunted from early morning until dusk, but could find nothing to eat. Hungry and tired, he sat down by the trail to rest, when along came Sungura, the hare, hop-skip, hop-skip, gay as a sunbeam.

"And what makes you so happy?" growled Fisi.

"It's been a good day for me, my friend. What is amiss with you?"

"You would be cross, too, if you had eaten nothing since yesterday. I'm starving, Sungura, simply starving."

Sungura looked closely at the hyena. He looked very hungry and tired as well. "Never mind, Fisi. You sit here and rest. I'll bring you some food."

"Oh, kind Sungura, what a friend you are," gasped the hyena as the hare hopped cheerfully away.

After a while Sungura returned with a gourd full of honey. "Honey!" cried Fisi, snatching the gourd and swallowing its contents in three tremendous gulps. "How delicious! Thank you, friend."

Sungura hopped away, marveling that anyone could eat so much honey so quickly.

Now the hyena lay down to sleep, but was soon awakened by a terrible stomach ache. Oh, how dreadful he felt! He lay on the ground moaning and groaning, making gruesome noises. These sounds were heard by the Kihuru bird, who happened to be flying by. He came down to investigate. "And what can be wrong with you?" he asked.

"Sungura brought me honey. It must have been poisoned," wailed the hyena. "I think I should have something else to eat to keep that honey from killing me."

"Very well, Fisi," said the Kihuru. "You just catch hold of my leg and I will fly with you over the mountain to a place where there are many fruits and honey and also much meat. You should find plenty to eat there."

"Oh, how wonderful," sighed the hyena. "There I shall never go hungry again." He caught hold of one leg of the huge bird and away they went.

When they were high over a mountain valley, Fisi saw a herd of goats below. "Let me down, Kihuru," he demanded. "I want one of those goats to eat."

"Wait," said the bird. "On the other side of the mountain there is more food."

"How do I know that? I'm stopping here." Fisi let loose of the bird's leg and went tumbling head over tail to earth. He landed with a tremendous bump, frightening all the goats away. When he arose, dazed and aching, he found that his leg was badly sprained. To this very day the hyena walks with a limp, all because he was greedy.

The Author

Eleanor B. Heady collected the stories for *Jambo, Sungura* during the years 1958–1959 when she traveled with her husband to East Africa, where he was engaged in grassland research. At the end of that time, they returned to the University of California at Berkeley, where he is professor of range management.

Mrs. Heady has long been interested in writing and literature. Born in Bliss, Idaho, she lived on a ranch in the Snake River Valley and began writing at the age of ten. After graduation from Bliss High School (with only seven classmates) she attended the University of Idaho at Moscow, where she received her B.A. in English in 1939. The next year she taught English and drama.

Since her marriage in 1940, Mrs. Heady has worked for a number of radio stations. In Bozeman, Montana, she was a staff announcer and had her own weekly children's program, for which she wrote most of the stories, and in California she has done storytelling for the educational radio station KPFA. Mrs. Heady's other recent activities include serving as chairman of the Writers' Workshop of the University of California and as secretary for the Committee for African Students, a volunteer group assisting young Africans with higher education. The Headys have a son and daughter.

The Artist

Robert Frankenberg is well-known as an illustrator of children's books, with more than sixty to his credit. He is currently head of the drawing department of the School of Visual Arts in New York City, and has been on the faculty since 1947.

Mr. Frankenberg was born in Mount Vernon, New York, and attended the Art Students League in New York City. He believes that "other things are as important to the illustrator as the more obvious tools of his trade; rich background in reading, an understanding of the period and location in which the story is set, an interest in the subject matter, careful and intelligent research, honesty of presentation." In his teaching, Mr. Frankenberg states that he tries to "give my students a definite direction based on the above principles, as well as regard for the individual student's talent and personality."

From 1941 to 1945 Mr. Frankenberg served with the U.S. Army. In addition to book illustration, he has worked for a number of magazines, and has had two one-man exhibits of his drawings in New York and several others throughout the United States. He is married and lives in New York City.